Albert's Thanksgiving

Picture books by
Leslie Tryon

Albert's Alphabet

Albert's Play

One Gaping Wide–Mouthed Hopping Frog

Albert's Field Trip

Dear Peter Rabbit
(written by Alma Flor Ada)

Albert's Thanksgiving

Albert's Thanksgiving

by Leslie Tryon

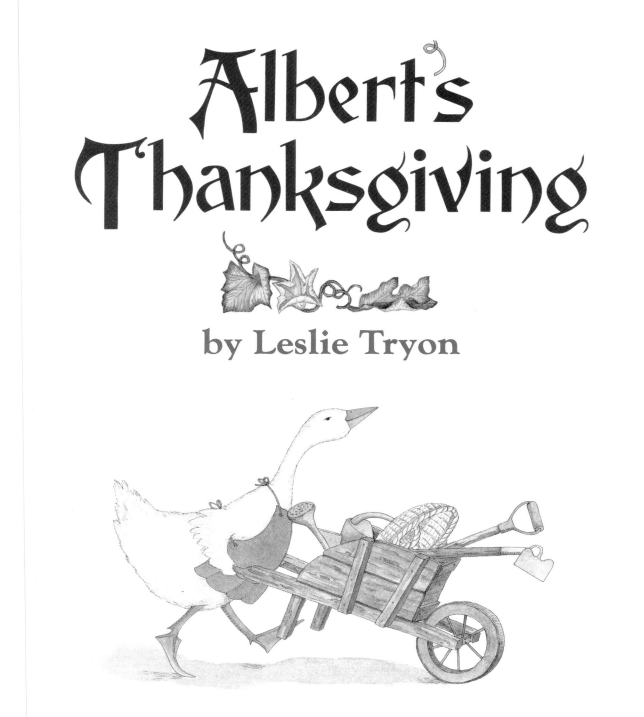

ATHENEUM 1994 NEW YORK

Maxwell Macmillan Canada
Toronto
Maxwell Macmillan International
New York Oxford Singapore Sydney

Special thanks to Con Pederson

Atheneum
Macmillan Publishing Company
866 Third Avenue
New York, NY 10022

Maxwell Macmillan Canada, Inc.
1200 Eglinton Avenue East
Suite 200
Don Mills, Ontario M3C 3N1

Macmillan Publishing Company is part of the Maxwell Communication Group of Companies.

First edition
Printed in Hong Kong by South China Printing Company (1988) Ltd.
10   9   8   7   6   5   4   3   2   1
The text of this book is set in Goudy Old Style.
The illustrations are rendered in watercolors and pen and ink.

Library of Congress Catalog Card Number: 94-8025

ISBN 0-689-31865-0

For Jon

Albert helped the children plant the garden. They cared for it together and watched it grow. Now it is time for the final harvest before their big Thanksgiving Feast...but everyone is so busy—who has the time? And will anyone remember?

Wednesday

Dear Albert,

Tomorrow is the P.T.A.'s Thanksgiving Feast. The children and I are working on the last-minute details.

There is just one little favor I'd like to ask you to do for us. We need a new table, and you're such a wonderful carpenter, I can't imagine anyone else building it. Can you find the time? I think it should look like this...

Thank you for your help
Patsy Pig
President, P.T.A.

After finishing the table Albert barely had time to pick a few carrots when he was interrupted with another note.

Dear Albert,

I hope you can find the time to help with just one more little thing.

The children are busy, busy, busy working on their pilgrim hats and Indian headbands, so they can't finish these cross-legged turkeys. I thought I would have time, but I'm just too busy. The pieces are all precut. Do hope you can find the time.

How are you doing with the new harvest table? Can't wait to see it.

Thank you,

Patsy Pig

Albert had just begun to pick the cauliflower when...

Hi, Albert — guess who,
    Will you be able to help us with just one more thing? My volunteers and I are terribly busy binding the cornstalks for the feast, so we really don't have the time to clean up the picnic area—will you do it? And, if you see any pretty, bright-colored leaves, please save them for the table decorations. And check the firepit—do we have enough firewood?

                    Patsy Pig

p.s. Are you finished making the new table and the cross-legged turkeys yet? You do such good work.

p.p.s. Since you'll be in the picnic area, will you be a dear and get the corn out of the corn crib? Just leave it in the cafeteria.

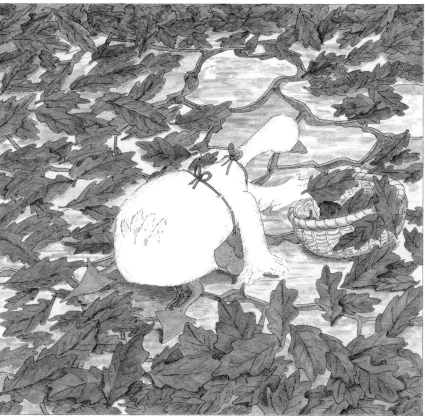

Oh no, not again!

Dear Albert,
    I hope you haven't forgotten
that you promised to make your
scrumptious pumpkin pizza pies for
the feast dessert—they're the
children's favorite! Be sure to
make plenty.
    I assume you will want to
make them this afternoon; I know
that I would. There won't be time
in the morning because of all the
other last-minute things we'll
have to do.

Ta,

Patsy Pig

p.s. Albert, you're just too too special.
The table and the cross-legged turkeys
look magnificent!

Oh no. Now what?

Al,

We're all just simply exhausted—what a day it has been. We've locked up the office and we're taking these tired children home for the night.

If I think of anything else we need, I'll tell you in the morning. I may need some help ironing all those pilgrim costumes; can't have our Thanksgiving without those, now can we?

Thanks,
P. P.

Albert,
We made a hat for you too.
♡ Gary

(Thurs.)

Good morning PTA,

Glad you like the table. I'm pleased you're pleased with the cross-legged turkeys. The corn is in the cafeteria. The picnic area is clean. I stacked the wood by the firepit. I gathered the leaves, and the pumpkin pizza pies are on the cooling racks. I've done every little thing you asked me to do. Glad to help. But did anyone think of the vegetables?

Thanks!

Albert

Finally! Patsy helped Albert pick the carrots and the cauliflower while the children gathered up every last head of nice fresh lettuce and cut all the flowers along the fence. Patsy picked the perfect pumpkin to use as a centerpiece. It was going to be a wonderful feast indeed.

Dear Albert,
  The Pleasant Valley School P.T.A. Thanksgiving Feast was a big success. Thank you for all the little things you did to help. I don't know what we'd do without you.

  Sincerely,
  Patsy Pig
  President, P.T.A.

p.s. Are you planting bulbs for the spring? I've got an idea for a spring flower show—I'll be in touch.